# POLAR

*by*
ELAINE MOSS

*Pictures by*
JEANNIE BAKER

Greenwillow Books
New York

*For Zara*

Text copyright © 1975 by Elaine Moss
Illustrations copyright © 1975 by Jeannie Baker
First published in Great Britain in 1975 by André Deutsch Limited
First published in the United States in 1990 by Greenwillow Books
All rights reserved. No part of this book
may be reproduced or utilized in any form
or by any means, electronic or mechanical,
including photocopying, recording or by
any information storage and retrieval
system, without permission in writing
from the Publisher, Greenwillow Books,
a division of William Morrow & Company, Inc.,
105 Madison Avenue, New York, N.Y. 10016.
Printed by Proost International Book Production, Belgium
First American Edition  10 9 8 7 6 5 4 3 2 1

Library of Congress Cataloging-in-Publication Data

Moss, Elaine.
Polar / by Elaine Moss : pictures by Jeannie Baker.
p.   cm.
Previously published: London : A. Deutsch, 1975.
Summary: A teddy bear's exploits in his toboggan
bring him injury, but also the attention of kind friends.
ISBN 0-688-09176-8. —ISBN 0-688-09177-6 (lib. bdg.)
[1. Teddy bears—Fiction.  2. Dolls—Fiction.  3. Tobogganing—
Fiction.]  I. Baker, Jeannie, ill.  II. Title. PZ7.M852Po 1990
[E]—dc19   89-2115   CIP   AC

This is Polar.
Most teddybears are yellow but he is
white as snow on a dark dark night.

He sleeps in a bed. With his friends Pam-Pam and Jack beside him he is not too afraid of the shadows, though Tiger prowls and Owl hoots and the bright white moon shines through the window.

Polar dreams of a land
where the slippery ice glistens in the sun,
the seals flop on their flippers
and only the fish have fun frolicking in
the deep waters below the thick ice.

"Wouldn't it be nice to feel some snow flakes in my fur?" sighs Polar as he opens his eyes. Then, to his surprise, he sees a hillside covered with snow.

Polar kicks back his quilt and dresses
himself in his warmest clothes: red woolly
trousers and the snug thick sweater he loves,
his striped hat with the pom-pom,
and his yellow mittens.

"Come tobogganing!" shouts Polar. But Pam-Pam
and Jack sneak back under the quilt.
Polar makes a toboggan from a box and some books.

Polar pulls his toboggan up the hill.

Polar sits in his toboggan.

"Shall we give you a push?" ask Pam-Pam
and Jack.
"No," says Polar. "I can go by myself,
you watch!"
Slowly he slides.
Then, skeltery-slither-whoosh-bumpetty

STOP!

And again, over the freezing snow.
Slow, slide, skittery, slither, whoosh, bumpetty
STOP!
It's easy!

Soon Pam-Pam and Jack hear Polar call,
"Do you think I can stand in my sled?"
Jack says, "No, you'll fall!"
But the bear doesn't care.
Not he!

"See!" cries Polar, nose high in the icy air.
"Here I go!"
But the sled hits a hump
and Polar comes tumbling
down, down, bump
down like a lump of timber:

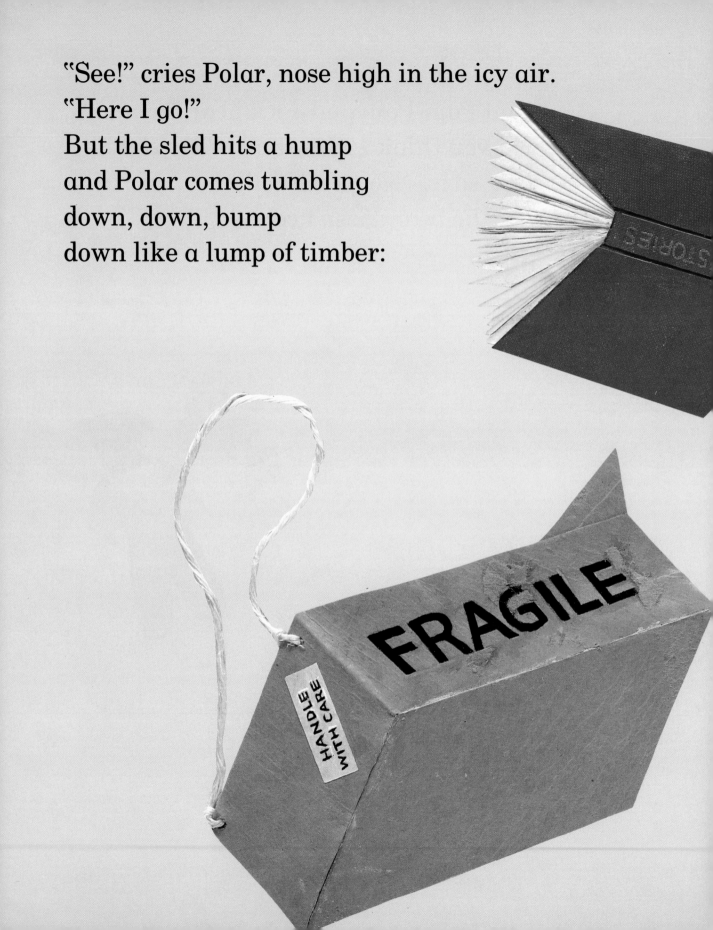

Numb, dumb bear.

Pam-Pam tries not to cry as she
binds Polar's wounds.
Jack says, "Fetch a book to make a stretcher.
Sh! He's fast asleep. We must go to the
hospital for help!"

Polar is not dead.
When he wakes he has a bandage on
his head, his leg is slung up in the
air to mend, and his arm won't bend.
But Pam-Pam and Jack are there to
comfort him.

His chair is full of presents from his
friends. Owl and Tiger have sent a jar
of the licky sticky honey he likes so much.

Soon he is limping around on crutches.

Then it is time to go home.